kale

sawbuck

red cent

greenbacks

smacker

Amelia

Works It Out

by Marissa Moss
(and here's-my-card Amelia)

two bits

dough

American Girl™

SCHOLASTIC INC.

New York Toronto London Auckland Sydney
Mexico City New Delhi Hong Kong Buenos Aires

cash

Professional Journal
Writer

Have pencil, will travel.

Amelia

bucks

Arf!

moolah

← walking the dog

really walking the dog

This notebook is dedicated
to Kathleen,
a very hard worker.

Yip!

ISBN 0-439-46136-7

12 11 10 9 8 7 6 5 4 3   2 3 4 5 6 7/0

Printed in the U.S.A.   09

First Scholastic printing, September 2002

Book design by Amelia

An Amelia® Book

Yawn!

These are my feet now, in regular, plain old shoes — but I'm working on changing that. I never used to think about my feet, as long as they were comfortable, but that was before LIGHTSCAPE/NIGHTSCAPE shoes were invented. Now everybody at school has them. Except me. And they're really cool!

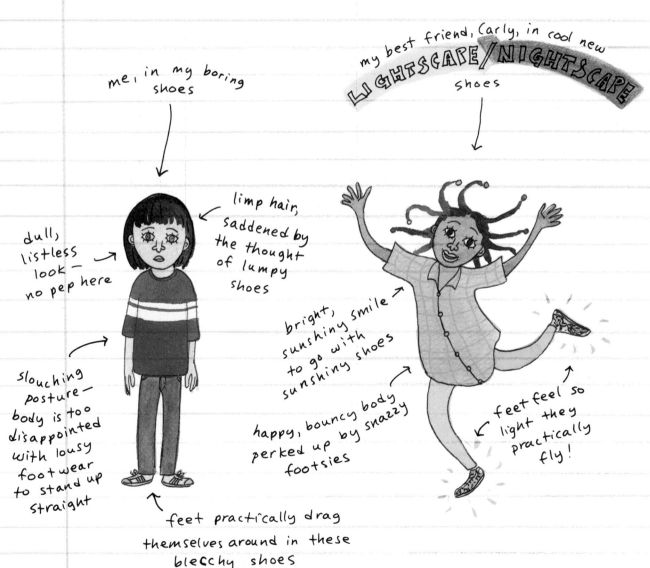

me, in my boring shoes

my best friend, Carly, in cool new LIGHTSCAPE/NIGHTSCAPE shoes

limp hair, saddened by the thought of lumpy shoes

dull, listless look — no pep here

bright, sunshiny smile to go with sunshiny shoes

slouching posture — body is too disappointed with lousy footwear to stand up straight

happy, bouncy body perked up by snazzy footsies

feet feel so light they practically fly!

feet practically drag themselves around in these blecchy shoes

Here's why **LIGHTSCAPE/NIGHTSCAPE** shoes are so neat-o!

They have a picture printed on them that's sensitive to light.

In the dark or low light, you see a night scene.

In strong light, it becomes a day scene.

There are all kinds of choices of pictures on the shoes.

a jungle

eek! eyes!

an ocean

glow-in-the-dark fish

too hot for animals in the day

cool enough to come out at night

a desert (not a dessert)

It's hard to decide which one's best.

This is dessert.

I mean, shoes like that are as close to magic as you can possibly get. I BEGGED Mom to get me a pair, but she said they're too expensive and that my old shoes are fine anyway.

I even pointed some out to her that were <u>on sale</u>. She still said no.

Oh, Mom, look!

Mom arm and sleeve ↓

Mom purse with the money I need →

I showed her how scuffed up my old shoes were, but she wasn't convinced.

old shoe, left foot (leave-behind shoe) ↓

Look at this shoe — it's worn out!

If there isn't a gaping hole, it's fine. <u>Wear</u> it outside, and <u>then</u> it'll be worn <u>out</u>.

I tried the angel act (after all, it worked when I wanted to go to Space Camp).

Your tea and cookies, madam!

Thanks, Amelia, but shoes aren't <u>educational</u> — Space Camp was.

↑ That's not true! I can learn a lot from shoes.

All that begging made Mom mad. She sent me to my room and told me to think of all the times I really wanted something but didn't like it after I actually got it. So here's my list of stuff that seems good at first but, when you think about it, isn't that great after all.

your name written on a grain of rice

in a little glass bottle like an incredible treasure

whose idea was this, anyway? And what if someone ate your name-rice by mistake?

Hmmm... extra crunchy!

silly eyeball headband

It's funny for about two seconds, then it's stupid.

talking toilet banks

Hey, lemme outta here!

You flush the coin down. Would you want to touch your money after it was in a toilet — even a toy toilet?

giant lollipop

This always looks so good, but after ten licks, you're sick of it.

light wand

It looks so pretty the first night, but the next day, all the little wires have fallen out and you just have a flashlight.

Even Carly tried to talk me out of wanting the shoes. Easy for *her* to say — she has some already!

My mom wouldn't buy them for me, either. My grandma did. But I didn't really care if I got them or not. It was *her* idea.

That was bad enough. Then the **WORST** happened. My own jelly-roll-nose sister got them. She bought them herself with money she earned babysitting.

Oh, Ameeeeeelia! I've got something to shoooooooow you!

Even **LIGHTSCAPE/NIGHTSCAPE** shoes can't transform *her* smelly old feet! I feel sorry for the shoes.

She picked the cityscape. That's the kind *I* want!

That does it! If Cleo can make enough money to buy them, so can I. Except I'm too young to babysit, so I'll have to think of something else. It's not fair that she gets paid to watch kids when I'd be much better at it. Why do people judge you by how old you are?

Cleo gets *everything* before I do — the clothes I wear, the bike I ride. If the only way I get **LIGHTSCAPE/NIGHTSCAPE** shoes is as a hand-me-down, I'll scream!

Things Cleo got to do before me:

lose a tooth
↓

ride a bike
↓

get an allowance
↳

go on a roller coaster
↑

spend a week at a sleep-away camp
↗

wear practically all my clothes — at least Mom doesn't
believe in hand-me-down underwear (socks are bad enough!)
↑

↖ earn money ↗

Since Mom won't buy me my shoes, I'll have to buy them myself.
What can I do to make money (preferably something Cleo hasn't done?)

Cleo said she'd pay me to clean her room — a whole 25¢. You'd have to pay me a LOT more than that to touch her gross, germy things. But she gave me a good idea for another way to earn money. I made a business card and slipped it under her door.

Guarantee Your Privacy!

Tired of being eavesdropped on when you have friends over? Worried your mom will hear about all the bad things you did? Then this is the PROTECTION you need! Pay Amelia the measly sum of $5 (that's right, folks, a mere $5!) and she will leave you utterly and completely ALONE!

No more ears under the door!

No more eyes peeping through the keyhole!

Unfortunately, Cleo didn't respond to my generous offer the way I thought she would. Instead she came storming out of her room and threatened to flatten me if I ever came near her door when she had friends over.

Cleo snorting with fury →

You little brat! I'll pay you good if I catch you spying on me!

← A knuckle sandwich isn't the payment I want.

So I need to think of another way to earn money. Anyway, I only have <u>one</u> sister. I need a job where I can get <u>lots</u> of customers.

I wrote to Nadia, my old best friend. (She's still my faraway best friend and Carly's my close-by best friend. Nadia always has good ideas.)

·FASHIONS OF THE SIXTIES·

Dear Nadia,
  You know I don't usually follow fads, but I <u>really</u> want a pair of LIGHTSCAPE/NIGHTSCAPE shoes. <u>Not</u> because everyone else is wearing them, but because I think they're so cool.
  I'm trying to figure out how to make money so I can buy them. It's not easy! Any suggestions?
          luv, Amelia
yours till the shoe buckles!

Nadia Kurz
61 South St.
Barton, CA
91010

FADS 20
BELL BOTTOMS

Carly gets paid to do extra chores, like washing windows or mowing the lawn, but <u>my</u> mom pays so little for that kind of thing, it would take FOREVER for me to earn enough.

me, old and gray by the time → I get my LIGHTSCAPE/NIGHTSCAPE shoes

still stooped over, even with cool shoes

Yee-haw! I finally got those shoes I've wanted for ages!

old-people size - do your feet shrink and wrinkle up the way your face does?

In the movies, when kids want to make money, they set up a lemonade stand. It was worth a try. Carly helped me juice the lemons. We added lots of sugar. Then, to make our lemonade special, I put in a few drops of blue food coloring. Carly wanted red, so she added some, and we ended up with purple lemonade. It looked _so_ cool! We got out some paper cups and made a sign, and we were open for business.

potential customers

Purple lemonade? Blecch!

Don't kids know that lemonade is supposed to be yellow — or pink?

You would think there would be crowds of people eager for a glass of our delicious purple lemonade. You would think there would be a line around the block. You would think we would sell at least 1 cup. We didn't. Not one!

lemon pucker →

way too full and sloshy →

FRESH COLD LEMONADE

25¢ a cup COME AND GET IT!

unfortunately, we drank all the lemonade we had left — definitely a BIG mistake!

lemonade bloat! my pants were ready to explode!

Business Lesson #1: It doesn't matter how great _you_ think the stuff you're selling is. If people don't want to buy it, you won't make money. It's like one of Ms. Busby's word problems in math class: if you make 25 glasses of lemonade at 25¢ a glass, but don't sell any, how much money do you make?

Zero! Nada! The Big Empty! Zip! Goose Egg! It all equals NOTHING!

At least I got a postcard from Nadia — <u>that's</u> something.

Dear Amelia,
 Those shoes must be
everywhere! I admit
they're cool, but I hate
to be like everyone else.
I wouldn't want people
to think I wore them
just to be one of the crowd.
And you know how my dad
feels about fads — no way he'd
get me a pair. Somehow I can't
spend my own money on clothes.

F A D S
PLATFORM
20 HEELS 20

amelia
564 North Homecrest
Oopa, Oregon
97881

luv, Nadia
yours till the
shoe polishes!

So I'm not the only person in the universe who doesn't have those shoes — Nadia doesn't either! That makes me feel a little better, but she's too far away for it to make a BIG difference.

Nadia didn't offer any job suggestions, but she probably thinks I shouldn't waste my money on shoes since she wouldn't. I don't want to spend money on clothes, either, but LIGHTSCAPE/NIGHTSCAPE shoes aren't just footwear — they're magic!

They seem so fun — like they could turn you into a happier, lighter, bouncier person. On TV, people fly in their amazing, beautiful shoes. I mean, I don't believe the commercials. I know shoes can't make you fly. But still, they do something to you. (Unless you're Cleo — then you're beyond LIGHTSCAPE/NIGHTSCAPE magic.)

I could PRETEND I'm flying in those shoes.

I tore this ad out of a magazine. I hope it's not the closest I get to owning a pair of LIGHTSCAPE/NIGHTSCAPE shoes.

LIGHT UP YOUR WORLD WITH LIGHTSCAPE/NIGHTSCAPE ™ SHOES!

Drinking a certain soda doesn't automatically make you cool. (But it _will_ make you burp!)

No matter what kind of shampoo you use, your hair will NOT bounce. (And why should you want it to bounce anyway? It's hair, not a ball!)

It may look delicious on TV, but you can _never_ make it taste that way at home.

I don't care how many mints you eat or how much gum you chew — if you want fresh breath, you still have to BRUSH YOUR TEETH!

Soap is soap is soap is soap is soap is soap is soap. It doesn't matter _which_ brand you use — it's still soap!

Who cares how soft toilet paper is? You're not sleeping on it!

Driving that new car will not make you rich, beautiful, and popular — but you won't have to take the bus.

All chocolates will melt in your hand.

The game on TV looks really cool because they add all this stuff around it that's not part of the game you get in the box.

It's not zany fun — it's just breakfast cereal.

Nothing you eat will really turn you into a superhero.

Fast-food joints don't mean it when they say they'll make food any way you want.

Maybe Nadia's right — I should just forget about LIGHTSCAPE/NIGHTSCAPE shoes.

At home I hear Nadia's voice inside my head.

Remember, it's not what you wear but who you are that matters.

But at school I hear other voices.

Here's how I yo-yo:

Don't you wanna be cool, like me?

Are you in or out?

What kind of person wears shoes like those?

① Leave yo-yo on table. Look! It's taking a nap!

At recess today I got an idea for a job that just might work. Carly, Maya, and I were jumping double Dutch, and so were a lot of other kids. But I noticed that most kids weren't jumping rope — they were playing with yo-yos. Personally, I'm not a great yo-yoer, but I am good at fixing them. And yo-yos need fixing if they're played with a lot.

yo-yo troubles

detached string

twisted-up string

gunk in between sides

② Swing yo-yo back and forth before someone's eyes — AMAZING yo-yo hypnotism!

So I decided to do yo-yo repair! Since I can't advertise on TV, I made business cards to pass out to possible customers.

③ Roll yo-yo along the floor while saying "Toooot toooot" — it's doing the choo-choo train!

← I gave out business cards like this one.

Making my business cards made me think about what the perfect job would be. I mean, there are some jobs that are so GREAT, I'd do them for <u>nothing</u>!

MORE DREAM JOBS

ICE CREAM
TASTER
~ yum, yum ~

Hmm, needs a touch more chocolate.

MOVIE REVIEWER

I give it a big thumbs-up! Good popcorn, too!

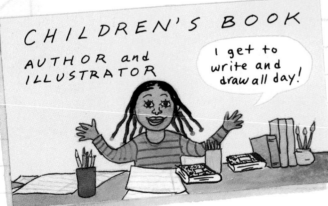

CHILDREN'S BOOK
AUTHOR and ILLUSTRATOR

I get to write and draw all day!

It looks like fun — and it is!

HOLIDAY WINDOW PAINTER

Then there are jobs I'd NEVER want to do, no matter what you paid me!

yo-yo repair tools

oil
replacement strings

soft cloth for polishing
really an old T-shirt

Fixing yo-yos may not be a DREAM job, but it's a job. I'm actually getting customers — LOTS of them! I couldn't charge a lot, though, or no one would hire me. So even though 9 kids asked me to fix their yo-yos, I earned a grand total of $13 (and one kid paid me with a comic book).

If this was a math problem, it'd go like this: Lulu earns 50¢ an hour mowing lawns. If she wants to save $50, how many hours will she have to work? Will she have time to do anything else?

poor, exhausted Lulu — worn out for a mere $6

Business Lesson #2: If you have a service people want, but they won't pay a lot of money for, you won't make enough money for it to be worth your time.

I want time to equal lots of money — not pennies.

sunny-side up clock or fried time → = or = ?

I've got to figure out something I can do that people want and that will pay me what I want.

 ← The comic book I got for cleaning Max's yo-yo was a good one, but it didn't get me any closer to buying my shoes.

Carly and I were walking home from school when I got an idea for a GREAT job.

We always pass this house with a little dog right next door to a house with a HUGE dog.

That gave me the idea — I could walk people's dogs! I like animals, I can walk, I'm not too young to hold a leash, lots of people have dogs but don't have time to walk them, and grown-ups will pay more than kids do — it's PERFECT!

I made business cards to advertise my new service. I'm calling it WOOF WALKERS. Carly helped me put my cards up all over the place — the library, grocery stores, post office, pet food store, anywhere dog owners might go.

WOOF WALKERS
No dog too big, no walk too long, no bark too loud.
Call Amelia, master dog-walker.

WOOF WALKERS
No dog too big, no walk too long, no bark too loud.
Call Amelia, master dog-walker.

since I put up my cards, I've been noticing dogs EVERYWHERE. I wonder which ones I'll get to wa[lk]

bald dog with giant ears →

little dust-mop dog →

squashed face dog →

Carly thinks my cards are really cute. She asked if I would make her a business card. She doesn't have a job yet, but someday she wants to be an investigative reporter.

I asked her to tell me about reporting so I'd know what to put on the card. →

It's important to ask the five W's — who, what, when, where, why. And don't forget the one with a W at the end — Ho w.

She's been a good friend to help me in my job searching. →

Carly's notebook
← She's always prepared to write something down.

Here are my five W's:
Why does Cleo get everything cool first? What can I do to earn money? Who will be my customers? Where will I find a job? When will I have my own LIGHTSCAPE/NIGHTSCAPE shoes? And how will it feel to finally wear them? I can't wait to answer that last question!

The business card I made for Carly looked like this.
She loved it! ↓

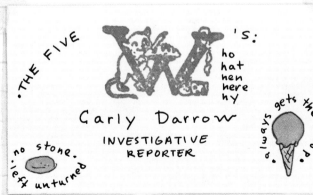

· THE FIVE W 's:
ho
hat
hen
here
hy
Carly Darrow
INVESTIGATIVE REPORTER
· no stone.
· left unturned
· always gets the scoop ·

But if anyone has noticed my dog-walking cards, I sure can't tell. No one's called to hire me yet. I'm waaaaiting!

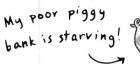
My poor piggy bank is starving!

side view of hollow piggy

↑ front view of hungry, caved-in piggy

I wish I didn't want those shoes so much. Getting work is just as hard as doing work.

It's so unfair that Cleo can earn money babysitting when all she probably does is eat popcorn and watch TV. I'm willing to really work, but no one will give me a chance. I'm not even asking to take care of kids — just dogs!

BURP!

Cleo's overfed piggy bank (really a hoggy bank!)

Cleo's idea of babysitting is sitting and stuffing her face.

Will you play Candy Land with me?

Go watch a video — I'm busy!

Tonight was the worst. She got home from her job chomping on leftover chow mein, and waved all this money in my face.

Mom says Cleo should save her money, but does she? No!!→

Hmmm... What should I buy next?

Let's count now...

Doggy business — what dogs do on walks: →

mmm!

← smell EVERYTHING!

Ah, aged sandwich crusts!

↑ eat gross things they find on the ground

Just as she was gloating, the phone rang and it was for me. I FINALLY GOT MY FIRST JOB !! WOOF WALKERS is in business! Mr. Singh wants me to walk Precious, his basset hound. He sprained his ankle (Mr. Singh, not Precious), so he can't do it for the next week or two. That means I have a job for 2 weeks, and he'll pay me $5 a day.

Another math problem:

2 weeks = 14 days, 14 days at $5 a day = $70 !
I'll be rich, rich, RICH!

Today was my first day at work. Maybe a long time ago Precious was precious, but now she's old and smelly. She's almost too old to walk. I feel like I'm dragging her down the sidewalk.

Arf, ARF, ARF!

↑ bark at anything that moves

C'mon, Precious. Don't you want a walky-poo?

← legs aren't moving at all

When I got home from pulling Precious, there was a message for me — another job! A guy down the street wants me to walk his terrier for a few days. Maybe the terrier will perk up Precious. It'll probably be easier to walk two dogs at once than drag one old dog like Precious.

The terrier's name is Yipster because she yips all the time. At least she's not old — she's definitely got pep!

I thought Yipster would make walking Precious easier, but it hasn't turned out that way at all. Precious _still_ doesn't want to go anywhere, but now I have Yipster pulling _me_ while I pull Precious. It would be funny in a cartoon, but it's not in real life.

arf arf arf arf arf arf arf arf arf arf arf

Also, Yipster chases cats, squirrels, and little kids, so I have to pull her away from something all the time. I'm getting very strong arms.

Just when I was getting the hang of walking two dogs at once, I got _another_ call. Ms. Friese from across the street asked me to walk her Irish setter this week because she has to work late. I didn't want to say no, because it means more money, but now I have _three_ dogs to walk. Well, I guess since I can handle two, one more won't make a difference.

more math:
$70 (Precious) + $25 (Yipster) + $35 (the Irish setter) = $130!! I've _never_ had that much money. I can buy my shoes and have lots of money left over!

By the time I got to Ms. Friese's house, I'd already imagined earning so much money, I didn't know what to do with it. I almost forgot that I had work to do first. Rusty reminded me right away.

Irish setters are BIG dogs.

Rusty was so excited to see me, he drooled all over my feet (good thing I was wearing regular old shoes).

Uh, down, boy, down!

I'm a small person.

With Rusty, Yipster, and Precious, I wasn't sure which dog to follow and which dog to pull in. Rusty decided for me — he was definitely going to lead. He ran so fast Yipster couldn't even yip. She had to save all her breath for keeping up with him. Precious, of course, didn't even try, but she weighed him down as much as she could. And me, I was somewhere in the middle, holding on to all their leashes so hard I got rope burns.

I was getting pretty tired of being walked (really "run") by Rusty instead of me walking him. Today when I walked the dogs, I decided things would be different. I didn't let Rusty yank me around — I started out with his leash really short and tight. We were walking, not running, very nicely (even Precious actually moved her legs once in a while) when

DISASTER STRUCK!!

Yipster saw a squirrel and, of course, started yapping and running after it. That got Rusty all excited. Then when he saw the squirrel, he really went wild! Rusty took off chasing it and, when it ran up a tree in someone's yard, he followed it. Rusty jumped over the fence into the yard, pulling all of us along. Yipster ran through the fence slats, Precious was dragged up against the fence, and I was left on the other side with her, yelling at the dogs to stop. They didn't stop. They barked like maniacs, plowing through the flower beds, racing around the tree. I thought things couldn't get worse — but they did!

There was a rake leaning against the tree. Rusty crashed into the rake, slamming it against a nearby window. **SMASH!** The window broke!

I stopped yelling, the dogs stopped barking. I couldn't believe it — now I was in BIG trouble!

A woman came out of the house, and she was REALLY MAD. I wanted to sink into the ground, but I had to just stand there and listen to her yell at me. I practically crawled home, I felt so bad. I would've quit right then, but I had to pay that woman back for the broken window and the crushed flowers.

I did make money. I got paid for all my jobs, but replacing those flowers and that window was expensive! After two weeks of hard work, I ended up with $11. That's worse than yo-yo repair!

Woof Walkers math problem: If you earn $130 in two weeks but your expenses are $119, what do you end up with? Is it less than $1 a day? If it is less, are you crazy?!

Business Lesson #3: Even if people will pay you a lot of money for your work, if the job costs you too much money, it's not worth it. (And it's definitely not worth it if it makes you miserable!)

O.K., I didn't make much money with my jobs, but there's one way I can get rich for sure — in a story! At least when I write things down, I can make them happen the way I want them to.

 WORKING WOES

Once there was a boy who had no money. Well, he had an allowance, but it wasn't very much. The problem was, he wanted money, he <u>needed</u> money, and he had no idea how to get it.

"Why don't you just print your own money," his friend suggested.

"But that's called counterfeiting. It's illegal. I'll go to jail," said the boy.

"I don't mean money that tries to look real," said his friend. "I mean money that's obviously fake. Funny money. You're a good artist. If you draw it really funny, people will buy it."

He made one-dollar bills

and twenty-dollar bills →

and zillion-dollar bills.

The boy thought it was a good idea, so he tried it.

He had a lot of fun making all his funny money.

People came from all over the world to buy his money. He gave them his drawings, and they gave him real money. He was rich, rich, RICH! And whenever he wanted more _real_ money, he just drew more funny money.

The End

I wish I were like that boy and could draw something to trade for what I want to buy. Or that I could draw the shoes and they would magically become real.

more math: 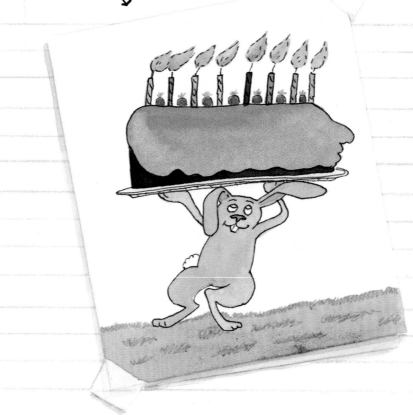 =

Carly said her dad loved the business card I made for her. Now she wants me to make a birthday card she can give to him. (She says she's a terrible drawer. She's so shy about it, I've never even seen her draw.)

I made a card like this.
↓

Cleo saw me drawing it, and I thought she'd make nasty comments like she always does. But she didn't — instead she said she'd PAY me to make a card for her to give Gigi, her best friend.

That's when the lightbulb went on! The best part of all my jobs was drawing business cards for them. If I make cards — <u>greeting</u> cards — for other people, I can get paid for what I have fun doing! I was so excited, I gave Cleo a big hug and kiss.

Thank you, thank you, thank you!

Geeez, I just wanted one little card.

Carly thinks my card idea is terrific. After school she went with me to the art store to get supplies. I used my yo-yo and **WOOF WALKERS** money to buy paper and envelopes.

art kit with artistic supplies →

glitter pens

colored pencils you can draw <u>and</u> paint with

Draw a line first.
↓

glow-in-the-dark paints

cool brushes in different shapes

Dip a brush in water and turn the line into paint!

I bought my paper, but what I really wanted was this cool art kit. Too bad I didn't have enough money for it. (That's the story of my life — I never have enough money for ANYTHING important — at least, not yet!)

With my new supplies I made cards, stationery, and postcards. I used my old pencils, markers, and paints. It was a lot of fun, and I love the idea that people might think my drawings are good enough to actually pay money for them!

Maybe next I can draw comic books, make copies at the copy store, and sell Amelia comics.

↙ handmade postcards — I sent one to Nadia and one to my Japanese pen pal

Wish...

Amelia's Art Cards

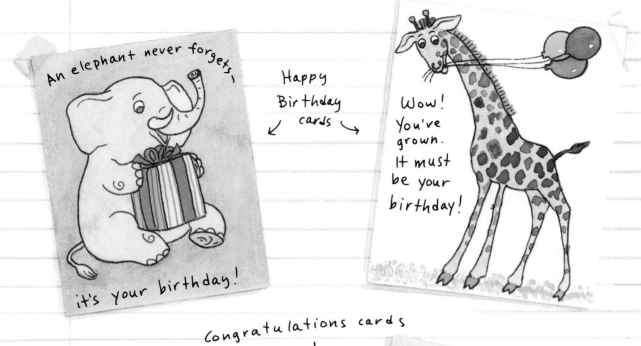

An elephant never forgets,

it's your birthday!

Happy Birthday cards

Wow! You've grown. It must be your birthday!

Congratulations cards

YOU DID IT!

fill in the blank

HOORAY FOR YOU!

Thank-you cards

You shouldn't have — but I'm glad you did!

Oooh! I love it!

I'm flying to tell you...

small so you don't have to write a lot

Since making cards was Cleo's idea, I gave her first pick. She chose a giraffe card for Gigi. I brought the rest with me to school.

I was showing them to Carly when Charisse came over and asked to see them. I always thought Charisse was perfect, but she says she's <u>not</u> a perfect drawer. She loved the bear card, so she bought it. My first sale! (Aside from family, which doesn't count).

Charisse showed my card to her friends, so at recess they wanted to get cards, too.

Look at mine!

Look at mine!

Susie bought one, and so did Angela.

By lunchtime, a lot of kids knew about my cards. Leah, who's a good artist herself, bought one.

I love it!

Max chose one.

Thanks!

Even one of the hairnet ladies wanted a birthday card.

Tasty drawing, hon!

After that, everywhere I went, someone asked for a card!

Hilary, who used to be so mean to me, paid me $1 for a thank-you card.

My teacher, Ms. Busby, bought 2 postcards!

Luckily I had one left for Mom to buy.

It's great, honey!

I DID IT!

I finally, _finally_, FINALLY earned enough money to buy my own LIGHTSCAPE/NIGHTSCAPE shoes! Carly and I are going to walk to the shoe store after school tomorrow so I can get them.

wallet bulging with hard-earned money

Even with my ordinary shoes, I feel like I'm walking on air!

I tried on a pair and they fit! I have to admit, my feet looked GREAT in those shoes. I really wanted them, really I did... at least I thought I did. But somehow when it was my turn in line and the cashier was ready to ring them up, I just couldn't buy them. I mean, I worked so hard for that money, I wanted to buy something really special with it. I thought that the LIGHTSCAPE/NIGHTSCAPE shoes were that special thing, but they weren't. Maybe all along I had wanted them just because everyone else had them.

Carly couldn't believe it.

After all that, you're not getting them?

After all that, I don't really want them.

Mom was right. Sometimes when you get something you've really wanted, you wonder why you ever wanted it in the first place.

And it's different when you have to buy it yourself instead of getting it as a present. →

It's hard to break your piggy bank ↑

But I did want something, and this time I was sure what that something was.

"C'mon," I told Carly. "Let's get what I've been saving for."

"I thought the shoes <u>were</u> what you were saving for," Carly said.

"Nope," I said. Carly looked at me like I was crazy, but she followed me down the block. We went into the right store this time, and I couldn't stop smiling when I paid for my brand-new, neato-mosquito

Carly smiled, too. ↓

Now *that's* smart! With the art kit, you can make more cards and earn *more* money.

I've got ideas for lots **more** cards!

↓

It's that time again!

↑

Birthday reminder cards, so people don't forget to send you presents.

I **LOVE** my art kit, and I've already made my first card with it. I gave it to Cleo. After all, she __was__ my first customer — one thing I didn't mind her being first at — and she gave me the idea.

It looked like this. ↓

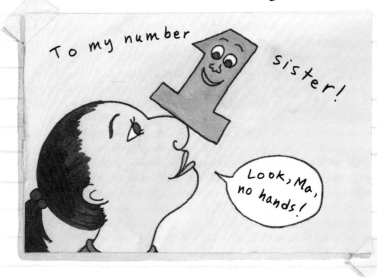

To my number 1 sister!

Look, Ma, no hands!

congrats! your braces are off!

Special occasions that people need to notice.

↓

YEAH! Your ears are pierced

Business Lesson #4: Find what you love to do, and get paid to do it!

I'll make up my own holidays.

↓

National Cookie Baking Day! Take a bite!

Or, to put it in a math problem:

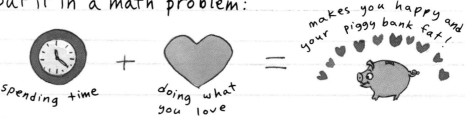

spending time + doing what you love = makes you happy and your piggy bank fat!

That's the kind of math I love!